Book Seven

WheN BuNNies TuRN Bad

or

The Sun-Ripe Raisin Man

A bit about the author

Philip Ardagh, whose very first **GRuBtoWN taLe** won him the Roald Dahl Funny Prize, is author of numerous books including the award-winning Eddie Dickens adventures, which have been translated into over 30 languages. He wrote BBC Radio's first truly interactive radio drama, collaborated with Sir Paul McCartney on his first children's book and is a 'regularly irregular' reviewer of children's books for the *Guardian*. Married with a son, he divides his time between Tunbridge Wells and Grubtown, where he cultivates his impressive beard.

GRuBtoWN taLes
Book Seven

WheN BuNNies TuRN Bad

or

The Sun-Ripe Raisin Man

by Philip Ardagh

Illustrated by Jim Paillot

ff

faber and faber

Typeset by Faber and Faber Limited
Printed in England by CPI Bookmarque, Croydon

A CIP record for this book
is available from the British Library

ISBN 978–0–571–27236–5

2 4 6 8 10 9 7 5 3 1

A bit about Grubtown

You won't find Grubtown on any maps. The last time any mapmakers were sent anywhere near the place they were found a week later wearing nothing but pages from a telephone directory, and calling for their mothers. It's certainly a town and certainly grubby – except for the squeaky clean parts – but everything else we know about the place comes from Beardy Ardagh, town resident and author of these tales.

GRuBtoWN taLes were made possible through the participation of the following people, animals and organisations:

THE GRUBTOWN
CHAMBER OF COMMERCE

THE GRUBTOWN
CHAMBER OF
HORRORS

THE OFFICE
*of the Mayor
of Grubtown*

OFFAL'S
SUNBEDS

THE SHED
*of the Mayor
of Grubtown*

*The Mayor
of Grubtown
Himself*

THE GRUBTOWN
RIFLE
CLUB

THE GRUBTOWN
TRIFLE
(& JELLIES)
CLUB

THE GRUBTOWN
POLICE
DEPARTMENT

KILL ALL DUCKS

Wretching's
Dairy

JIP
THE PELICAN
★ ★ ★
GRUBTOWN'S
OFFICIAL
MASCOT

GRUBTOWN
COASTGUARD
& DECKCHAIR
DEPARTMENT

THE RUSTY
DOLPHIN CAFE

CONTENTS

A Message from Beardy ARdagh

This is the seventh full-length **GRuBtoWN TaLe** and is unusual because it doesn't have Jilly Cheeter or Mango Claptrap in it. I know they both appear on the cover, but that's a trick. That's to make fans of Jilly Cheeter and Mango Claptrap go, 'Oh, goodie! Jilly Cheeter and Mango Claptrap are in this one too!' and then BUY a copy . . . only to get home and find that they've been fooled, by which time it will be too late. The booksellers will have put their money in their sacks and taken it to the bank and won't give them a penny back. Ha! Ha!

So, instead of Jilly Cheeter and Mango Claptrap, the main character in this

GRuBtoWN taLe is called Failing Toucan, a depressing boy who spends most of his time sobbing with a finger up his nose.

And nothing much happens.

ENJOY!

Beardy Ardagh

Grubtown

The inhabitants of Grubtown

At the back of the book (starting on page 129), you'll find a list of people living in Grubtown. You might find it useful if you want to buy them all presents. If you don't want to buy every Grubtowner a present, perhaps you could start alphabetically, beginning with people whose second name begins with the letter 'A', such as – er – Ardagh. Beardy Ardagh. Yes, that's a good idea. (*Publisher's note:* Beardy Ardagh *made* us write this bit. We didn't want to.)

A further message from Beardy Ardagh

I was lying. OF COURSE Jilly Cheeter and Mango Claptrap are in this seventh **GRuBtoWN taLe**. They were in the thick of things when the bunnies turned bad, so how could I tell the story without them? But the part about paper aeroplanes I mention on the back cover? I made that up! (Do you think I'll get into trouble?)

Chapter One
Branching out

Jilly Cheeter was hanging upside-down like a bat. Her best friend, Mango Claptrap, was hanging upside-down like an idiot.

'You look like an idiot!' Jilly Cheeter laughed.

'You look like a bat!' said Mango Claptrap.

They were both hanging from Manual Org's tree. Manual Org had been living in this particular tree for many years but only in the last few years had it looked so *sparkly*.

The reason? It now had enormous diamonds hanging from it likeVERY expensive Christmas-tree decorations.They glinted in sunlight (when it was sunny) and they glinted in lantern light (when there were lanterns about, giving off light) . . .

. . . and it was in lantern light that the dangly diamonds were now all glinting as Jilly Cheeter and Mango Claptrap swung side-by-side on one of the lowest branches.

Manual Org was standing at the foot of the tree, wearing one of his very favourite wigs. It was very blonde and very straight. Manual Org used to have some very greasy hair of his own but nowadays he's as bald as a cabbage (unless you come from somewhere where cabbages are very hairy). He was sipping slerch, his favourite drink, from his favourite mug (with the picture of the four-leafed lucky clover on it).

'Mind you don't fall—' he said, just as Mango fell to the ground with a **THUMP**, narrowly avoiding a passing bunny (which hopped to safety).

'Are you all right?' asked Jilly Cheeter, swinging down and landing on her feet.

'Never felt better,' said Mango, which was almost true. He rubbed his head. It felt a tiny bit painful – but nowhere near as painful as the time when the clock from **THE GRUBTOWN AQUARIUM AND CARWASH** had landed on him – but otherwise he was feeling quite tickety-boo. (Mango Claptrap liked the word 'tickety-boo' ever since he'd heard town know-all Informative Boothe use it the previous week, and loved to say it himself at every opportunity. In fact, *saying* 'tickety-boo' made him feel even *more* tickety-boo, which was nice.)

Life for Jilly Cheeter and Mango Claptrap was good. Jilly no longer had to get up early and go to bed late (unless she wanted to) because she was no longer Grubtown's official duck-gatherer.

She hadn't wanted the job of gathering up the town's ducks and putting them to bed in The Duck House (for their own safety). Her dad had sent her to the council offices to complain about their neighbours having a cane toad living in their compost heap and their not having one for themselves . . . but she'd gone through the wrong door, which is easily done. (Most of the doors inside the Town Hall look very much like the other doors, except for the ones which Mayor Flabby Gomez has to go through a lot. These ones are DOUBLE doors. Even though he's not as big as his dad, Big Man Gomez, was, he's still impressively w–i–d–e.)

Jilly Cheeter had ended up in the office of Rambo Sanskrit, Grubtown's official job-giver-outer and – before she could say 'Actually, I'm here about an amphibian!' – she'd found herself being handed a duck-call whistle and the key to The Duck House. And so had begun her time as guardian of the town ducks (mainly protecting them from the evil-doings of the duck-hating Fox family).

But that was then.

And this was now.

★ ★ ★

Like most people in the world, most people in Grubtown are perfectly nice. They may be annoying sometimes, by:

- talking when you wish they'd be quiet
- sitting in silence when you want a good natter
- trying to force bowls of nourishing soup on to you when all you want to do is sit quietly in the corner sucking the end of your tie
- spending too long stroking the guinea pig when they *know* it's your turn now
- treading on your beard

. . . but, most of the time, most Grubtowners are perfectly decent townsfolk. I'm not including the Fox family, of course. They drive me bonkers. No, they drive me more than bonkers. They drive me up the wall, stop for petrol, start off again – pulling straight out into traffic without looking left or right – *then* drive me all the way to bonkers and back again. Here, let me draw you a diagram:

See?

But the most annoying person by far, and no one in Grubtown would argue with me on this point (except, perhaps for the man himself) is Wide Brim Petty-Mandrake.

Petty-Mandrake used to be married to

Mrs Petty-Mandrake but one day she finally had enough and ran out of the house, never to return. She didn't even hang around long enough to pack a bag, in case Wide Brim Petty-Mandrake appeared and suddenly started complaining about the colour of water, or how trees weren't as good as they used to be, or how bunnies' tails don't really look as white and round and fluffy as they do in cartoons. Instead, she grabbed just two things: her collection of interesting matchbooks (not to be confused with matchboxes) and their son, Tie-Pin.

Wide Brim Petty-Mandrake didn't miss the matchbooks (not to be confused with matchboxes) — he'd always worried that they might be a fire hazard and end up burning the whole house down — but he did miss Tie-Pin. Fortunately, the boy comes to visit his father in Grubtown quite often. Fortunately for Grubtown, young Tie-Pin Petty-Mandrake is NOTHING like his dad.

It was Tie-Pin Petty-Mandrake who ambled into view, hands in pockets, as Jilly Cheeter, Mango Claptrap and Manual Org stood bathed in lantern light at the foot of the glinty tree. He'd just wandered across a patch of scrubland – officially called **THE WASTE OF SPACE** but known by us locals as 'the patch' – which, on the evening in question, seemed

to have rather a large number of big, white bunnies lolloping around in it. Next, he'd crossed the not-quite-so-new-now new Flimsy Bridge, so was feeling a little queasy.

Even when the wind is as weak as it was that day – like a really puffed-out smoker – Flimsy Bridge moves in a rather worrying way.

I've lost a lot of weight since I wrote the first of these **GRuBtoWN taLes** and, at the time of these events, I was over five stone lighter than I was back in the days when Manual Org was the most repulsive man in town. But, even as the new lighter-weight Beardy Ardagh, you wouldn't catch me crossing Flimsy Bridge. I have a nasty feeling that there'd be that moment – popular in cartoons – when I'd look down, suddenly realise that the bridge had fallen away, see that I was walking in mid-air and then fall through the sky with an 'Aaaaaaaaaaaarrrrrrrrrrrrrrrrghhhhhh!!!'

Tie-Pin Petty-Mandrake was made of sterner stuff. 'Hi, Jilly. Hi, Mango. Hello, Mr Org!' he said.

'Hello, Tie-Pin,' said Manual Org. 'When did you get back in town?'

'Last night,' said Tie-Pin Petty-Mandrake. 'Mr Grumbly picked me up from the airport.'

As well as being the father of the well-known Grumbly girls – the terrible singing sisters – Chester Grumbly is also one of Grubtown's finest taxi drivers. He knows where most places are. He doesn't overcharge and, unlike that woman with the hairy knuckles who drives for DUMP CARS, he doesn't eat Chinese meals at the wheel whilst driving. (Dump is the name of our second-nearest river, if you don't count the River Werty, which we don't in Grubtown because it shares its name with the village of Werty which isn't as good as our town.)

'How's your mum?' asked Jilly Cheeter.

'Fine thanks,' said Tie-Pin Petty-Mandrake. 'She's learning to make pots.'

'That's useful,' said Mango Claptrap. 'You can never have too many pots.'

'We have three hundred and forty-seven of

them,' said Tie-Pin. 'So far. And not all of them leak.'

'Great!' said Mango Claptrap.

'Brilliant,' said Jilly Cheeter.

'So what have you guys been up to since I saw you last time?' asked Tie-Pin. 'Have you two been given any more medals by the mayor lately?'

Jilly Cheeter was about to answer when there was a loud screech, like the laugh you'd expect from a chimpanzee (if you were expecting a chimpanzee), and an ape swooped down out of the branches and snatched the mug of slerch Manual Org had been sipping from.

They all four looked on in amazement.

'Coo!' said a passing pigeon, who was up late for a bird.

'Gosh,' said Mango Claptrap

'Blimey!' said Jilly Cheeter. 'You don't

see something like that
every day.'
She wasn't wrong.

Chapter Two
Monkeying about

You didn't have to be Informative Boothe to guess where the chimp came from. The animal had escaped from somewhere, and Grubtown doesn't have a zoo. There wasn't a circus in town at the time, and there was a very good reason for that. The very good reason is the Grubtown Circus Ban which has been in force ever since Alvin Backdraft was eaten by that tiger.

I don't want you to get all teary-eyed and upset at the thought of a tiger getting a terrible tummy upset from eating a human being, so let me quickly reassure you that the poor beast didn't eat ALL of Alvin Backdraft. Just his right arm.

Unfortunately for Alvin, he was right-handed. Fortunately for Alvin, he still has a left hand and has since learnt to write with that one instead.

The tiger's name was Rory and he had been supposed to stand on a stool in the middle of the circus ring but, instead, wandered over to Alvin Backdraft who'd just climbed into the ring and unrolled a banner which read:

Moments later, it read:

LACE FOR ANIMALS IS
HE WILD
T IN A CIRCUS

because Rory had taken a big bite out of it, along with that right arm of Alvin Backdraft which I mentioned a moment ago.

The very next day, Mayor Flabby Gomez and Chief Grabby Hanson announced that there would be no more circuses in Grubtown. Alvin Backdraft was not only a close personal friend of the mayor, it was also his job to wrap all of Grubtown's official parcels – his actual job title being Grubtown's official-parcel-wrapper-upper – which was something that was MUCH harder to do with one arm. Mayor Gomez was furious.

So with no Grubtown Zoo, and circuses banned from Grubtown, where had the chimpanzee in Manual Org's tree come from? If you're thinking that he might have escaped from the **Doohickey & Squat** science labs over in Werty, I'm going to award you extra points for being so smart. That's not the right answer, but some other well-known Grubtown animal residents – the rats who used to share the eight-storey-high garden shed with Flabby Gomez and his family before he moved into his knitted home – came from there, so it's GOOD THINKING. Well done, but don't get too big-headed. Nobody likes a big-head.

In truth, the chimp came from **THE GRUBTOWN HOME FOR OLD FOLKS**. He wasn't one of the residents, although he did have more than a passing resemblance to Global Tarp who is so old that he can remember the days before 'knock-knock' jokes (because no one had invented the door yet).

The chimp – who'd been named 'Clack' by Asphalt Nosegay, who owns and runs the home – was a petting pet.

Asphalt Nosegay used to get a magazine called **OWNERS OF OLD FOLKS' HOMES WEEKLY.** It came out every week and was for people who owned old folks' homes. In the third-week-of-July issue (which came out in the first week of September in this particular year), there was an article about how good it was for residents in old folks' homes – in other words: old folk – to have a pet to cuddle and stroke. According to the article, loving a pet had 'real therapeutic value'.

Asphalt Nosegay wasn't exactly sure what that last part meant, but she decided there and then – or maybe six minutes later – that she would get a pet for the residents of **THE GRUBTOWN HOME FOR OLD FOLKS**.

Something cheap.

The cheapest pet she could find at

SLY GUPPY'S PET EMPORIUM

was a goldfish. She thought it was rather pretty, but didn't think it would like being petted much, so she had to think again.

She decided against a hamster (after one bit her), wasn't sure how to spell 'guinea pig', and was just about to settle on a puppy – perhaps she thought it was a cushion – when Sly Guppy warned her, and she avoided flattening the poor thing at the last minute. Just then, the chimpanzee ambled in off the street.

'How much?' asked Asphalt Nosegay.

Now, the truth be told, Sly Guppy had never seen the chimpanzee before in his life so, technically, that meant that he had no right to sell the animal. But Sly Guppy likes money. I know this for a fact because once I was walking through **LOTS-OF-TREES WOOD** when I saw him outside his little cottage singing 'I like money!' and doing a funny little dance. Or was that Rumpelstiltskin? (I think it must have been Rumpelstiltskin. Sly Guppy doesn't live in a little cottage in the wood but in an apartment above the bicycle-repair shop in Tilt Street.)

So Asphalt Nosegay bought the chimp-who-wasn't-really-Guppy's-to-sell from Sly Guppy, named him 'Clack' and took him back to **THE GRUBTOWN HOME FOR OLD FOLKS**. Clack soon settled in. In less than a week, he not only had the best armchair in the TV lounge but he also had control of the

TV remote which would have made him the most important person in the room, if he were a person . . .

Only now he was in Manual Org's tree, drinking Manual Org's slerch.

'It's the ape from the old folks' home!' said Tie-Pin Petty-Mandrake. 'I wonder what he's doing here?'

'Drinking my slerch!' said Manual Org, which was whatever the opposite of a lie is. (Oh, yes: the truth.) 'Somebody should give Asphalt Nosegay a call and get her to come and collect him.'

'We could always take him back ourselves,' suggested Mango Claptrap. The boy was now sitting on the lowest branch

29

of the tree, wearing one of Manual Org's wigs, just for the fun of it. It was bright orange and very curly. If you were to meet someone whose real hair actually looked like that you'd probably think they'd been involved in an accident with some of Acrid Scorn's chemicals.

'We'll have to catch him first,' Jilly pointed out.

'Catch Asphalt Nosegay?' asked a slightly puzzled Tie-Pin Petty-Mandrake.

'No, the chimp!' said Jilly Cheeter and Mango Claptrap together as one.

'Oh,' said Tie-Pin.

'I seem to remember the animal's name is Clack,' said Manual Org, who often visits the old folk at the old folks' home to give them nuggets of gold or free trips to Wandaland. (Manual Org is not only very rich, you see, but also VERY NICE.)

'Here, Clack!' Tie-Pin Petty-Mandrake said to the chimpanzee.

Clack the chimp drank a final slurp of slerch – with a slerching noise – threw the empty mug over his shoulder, and then waddled over to Petty-Mandrake in that bow-legged chimpanzee kind of way. He held the boy's hand.

'Ah!' said Manual Org. 'Isn't that sweet.'

'He smells of pumpkin pie,' said Tie-Pin Petty-Mandrake, with some surprise.

'So does the Grubtown Home for Old Folks,' said Manual Org, 'which is why I always leave the place feeling so hungry. I usually dash round to the Rusty Dolphin for a quick bite to eat after a visit.'

Jilly Cheeter was already the other side of Clack, taking the chimp's other hand. Mango, meanwhile, was sitting up, and rubbing his forehead under the orange curly wig. He'd just been knocked off his branch by a low-flying mug.

'Let's go!' said Jilly Cheeter.

'It's getting late,' said Manual Org, in the flickering lantern light. 'Are you sure you wouldn't rather I phoned the home and asked someone to collect him?'

'It's fine,' said Mango Claptrap. 'The old folks' home is on my way home anyway, and Jilly is staying the night.'

'My dad is over in Limp helping fix the bouncy chicken,' Jilly Cheeter explained. The bouncy chicken over in the town of Limp is like a bouncy castle just about anywhere else, but chicken-shaped. Sloop Cheeter had been asked over to help try to repair a slow leak which had been caused when the bouncy chicken was hired off the Limp Chicken Society for a GRUNTING HedgePIGs gig. As the musically-minded amongst you probably already know, fans of the pop group GRUNTING HedgePIGs often dress up as purple hedgepigs (another name for hedgehogs), which means spiky clothes . . . and spiky clothes and bouncy chickens don't mix.

Sloop Cheeter wasn't asked over to help with the repairs because he's particularly good at repairing punctures. No, Sloop Cheeter was asked over to help to repair the punctures in the bouncy chicken because he has one of the biggest puncture repair kits for miles and MILES around. (If you thought Marley Gripe's puncture repair kit was big, you should see Sloop Cheeter's!)

And, because Jilly Cheeter only lives with her dad and their dog, Harvey, and they were away, she'd arranged to stay with the Claptraps.

Jilly Cheeter and Mango Claptrap thanked Manual Org for the drinks, Mango slipped off the wig and popped it in the nearest of the many wig-boxes – watched by a bunny from a nearby rabbit hole, eyes glinting in the lamplight – and they headed off with Tie-Pin Petty-Mandake and Clack the ape into the night.

It's not that far from Manual Org's tree to **THE GRUBTOWN HOME FOR OLD FOLKS**. It shouldn't take long to get from one to the other if you know the best way, don't get lost in the dark and don't have a chimpanzee which keeps wandering off, jabbering in that teeth-baring, excited-ape kind of way as though it was looking for someone or something.

If, however, you're not really sure of the best route – even if you think you do – and you do get lost in the dark and you DO have a chimpanzee with you which keeps wandering off . . . you can find yourself not exactly *lost* but not exactly sure where you are either. Which is exactly what happened to Cheeter, Claptrap and Petty-Mandrake.

After they'd been wandering around in the dark for about an hour longer than they would have liked to have been, Tie-Pin Petty-Mandrake made a suggestion.

'I think we should knock on someone's door and explain that we're sort-of lost,' he said.

'Good idea!' said Jilly Cheeter.

'Just what I was thinking,' said Mango Claptrap.

'There is one thing, though,' said Jilly Cheeter.

'No doors,' said Mango Claptrap.

'No houses,' said Jilly Cheeter. 'We haven't passed a single building –'

'Apart from that abandoned cheese store,' Mango Claptrap reminded her.

'– apart from that abandoned cheese store –

in the past half-hour.'

'Oh,' said Tie-Pin Petty-Mandrake. He looked worried (not that the other two could see that he looked worried in the blackness of the night).

'I'm sure we'll find someone soon enough,' said Jilly, who was finding it hard enough to find her own hand in front of her face. (It was that dark.)

Just then, all three heard a very friendly sound. It was *quacking*. There are few sounds friendlier than the quack of a duck except, perhaps, the quacks of several ducks. The more the merrier. But imagine how even-more-delighted Jilly Cheeter must have been, what with having worked with ducks for years and some of her best friends being ducks.

'Why aren't they all safely tucked up in The Duck House?' Mango Claptrap wondered out loud.

QUACK!

'Good point!' said Jilly. 'Perhaps they're having a party.'

It was as she said the word 'party' that Tie-Pin Petty-Mandrake fell into the lake. It was quite a shock for Jilly Cheeter and Mango Claptrap to hear the sudden 'SPLASH!' followed by Tie-Pin's cry of surprise, but not nearly as shocking as it was for the Petty-Mandrake boy himself.

One minute he'd been on dry land, listening to the quack of ducks in the pitch black and the next he'd stepped into deep water. It shouldn't have been a total surprise, I suppose. Ducks and water go together like Mango Claptrap and

SPLASH!

QUACK?

QUACK!

ridiculously short shorts or, say, salt and pepper
. . . but, when you're lost in the dark, you're
probably not thinking straight.

The sound of the splash got Clack the chimp
gibbering.

'Help!' shouted Tie-Pin,
followed by a bubbly swallowing-
water kind of sound.

The sound of Tie-Pin calling for
help made the ape gibber even more.

Both Jilly Cheeter and Mango Claptrap
wanted to help, of course, but they couldn't
even see him, let alone find a handy
branch for him to grab hold of.
They decided that, perhaps,
they should shout 'Help!'
too. Three people shouting
'Help!' was probably more likely
to attract attention than one (especially when
one of the three kept swallowing water).

And help did come, surprisingly quickly.

Chapter Four
Raisin to the rescue!

Jilly Cheeter and Mango Claptrap suddenly found themselves bathed in the brilliant white light of a very powerful torch. The man holding the torch was holding a silver-topped cane in the other hand. His face was hidden in the shadows, but the silver knob of the cane appeared to be carved into the shape of a grinning wrinkly fruit. He thrust out the cane, stabbing the end through the surface of the lake. 'Grab hold of this!' he shouted.

Tie-Pin Petty-Mandrake didn't need

asking twice. Blinking in the brilliant light he managed to hold on to the cane, and the man — with a little help from Jilly Cheeter and Mango Claptrap — heaved the bedraggled boy on to dry land. The chimpanzee made encouraging noises from the sidelines, and jumped up and down as if he was on an invisible pogo stick.

Tie-Pin sat in the one pool of light in the acres of darkness, dripping on to the grass.

'We'd better get you out of those wet things,' said the man. 'Follow me!'

Jilly Cheeter caught sight of his face in

the white torchlight. She gave a little gasp of surprise. He looked so wrinkled – so *strange* – yet so familiar and somehow so friendly.

Then Jilly suddenly realised why.

The man who'd appeared out of darkness in the middle of nowhere was none other than the Sun-Ripe Raisin man. You know: the Sun-Ripe

Raisin man!!! Or, to be more accurate, he was 'the face of Sun-Ripe Raisins' ('The Raisins That Are A Reason For Living') in the same way that Shoona Loose is the face of 'Frumple Fashion' or Sandy Garbfarb is the face of 'Lank Soaps'. The only difference being that Shoona Loose is also a movie star and Sandy Garbfarb is one of the best-known twelve-fingered golfers in the golfing world. Jilly Cheeter, however, only knew the face of Sun-Ripe Raisins – the Sun-Ripe Raisin man – as being just that: the Sun-Ripe Raisin man. She didn't think she'd ever seen him in a film or on a television programme or in a magazine or anywhere else . . . until now: in brilliant torchlight by a lake, as wrinkled as a raisin in real life as on television.

'You're Rumpus Corncrake!' Mango Claptrap blurted. He'd also recognised the man but had – impressively – managed to put a name to the (extraordinary) face.

'Indeed I am!' said Rumpus Corncrake.

'Now,' he said to Tie-Pin, 'we'd better get you into the warm.'

'The warm' in this instance turned out to be a wooden shack. It was nothing like the eight-storey garden shed Mayor Flabby Gomez had lived in with his family – and the Grubtown rats – while he'd been knitting his new house. The Sun-Ripe Raisin man's wooden shack really was just that: a wooden shack. It was one big room, which served as his living room, bedroom and kitchen, with a small bathroom walled off in one corner. But it was warm.

Part of what made it warm was the cast-iron stove with a little glass door at the front, through which Jilly Cheeter could see the red glow of burning wood. There was also the fact that the shack was full of white bunnies, hopping in, over, on, under and around anything and everything. (It reminded Jilly of her days working at the duck-filled Duck House.) Their furry little bodies were giving off heat like a living blanket

of twitchy-pink-nosed loveliness.

'Why so many bunnies, Mr Corncrake?' asked Mango Claptrap.

'They're nothing to do with me,' said the Sun-Ripe Raisin man. 'They simply turned up the other day. Perhaps they're attracted to my vegetable garden. 'Now I've more time on my hands, I've been growing a lot of veg . . .' He was busy rummaging in the middle drawer of a battered old chest of drawers. He pulled out a thick woolly blanket, revealing a dopey-looking bunny who peered at him with a pair of dopey pink bunny eyes before lolloping out of the drawer to take up residence under a footstool. Corncrake handed Tie-Pin Petty-Mandrake the blanket. 'Wrap yourself in this,' he said, 'and sit by the fire. Now, whose parents do I need to call to let them know where you all are, and to have them come and collect you?'

A quarter of an hour later – or fifteen minutes later, if you're using Grubtown time

– Jilly Cheeter, Mango Claptrap, Tie-Pin Petty-Mandrake and Rumpus Corncrake were chatting away happily around the stove, sipping hot chocolate. Corncrake had even managed to find a piece of bubble wrap for them to pop a couple of bubbles each. (Drinking hot chocolate and popping bubble wrap is one of our favourite pastimes here in Grubtown. We're simple folk with simple pleasures.)

Clack the chimp was sitting in the man's lap as though they'd known each other for years. They'd occasionally look at each other and grin.

'I didn't know you lived in Grubtown, Mr Corncrake,' said Jilly Cheeter.

'I never think of people on TV living anywhere, except for on TV,' admitted a shivering Tie-Pin Petty-Mandrake.

'I haven't lived here that long,' Rumpus Corncrake explained, 'and I didn't particularly want to advertise my presence. I've retired, you see, and will soon be mov—'

'You mean you're no longer the Sun-Ripe Raisin man?' Mango Claptrap gasped.

'I suspect I shall ALWAYS be the Sun-Ripe Raisin man,' Rumpus Corncrake replied. 'Even if I go on to star in a series of blockbusting movies or win awards for appearing on stage, the day I'm hit by a bus the papers will say "Sun-Ripe Raisin man dies".'

'You're planning to be hit by a bus?' asked a confused Tie-Pin.

'I mean that I've been typecast,' said Rumpus Corncrake. 'I mean that whatever I've done on stage in the past and whatever I do in the future, I will always be remembered for appearing in those advertisements . . . Then again, with a face as wrinkled as mine, I'm only really fit to play a raisin.'

'But they're good adverts,' said Jilly Cheeter.

'And Sun-Ripe Raisins are delicious!' added Mango Claptrap.

The Sun-Ripe Raisin man's crinkled face

broke into a smile. 'You're very kind,' he said. 'And I shouldn't complain. Before I became the Sun-Ripe Raisin man I spent years being anonymous on stage. I don't really have an *actor's* face, you see –'

'And appearing in the raisin ads has made you a household name!' said Mango Claptrap, who was busy checking that there wasn't a single unpopped bubble anywhere on the sheet of bubble wrap.

'More of a household person-in-a-certain-set-of-clothes than a household name,' said the actor, perhaps a little sadly. 'The name the Sun-Ripe Raisin people want you to remember is Sun-Ripe Raisins . . . not Rumpus Corncrake.'

'But I knew you were called Rumpus Corncrake, Mr Corncrake!' Mango Claptrap reminded him.

'But you're no ordinary boy!' said Rumpus Corncrake, looking at Mango in his ridiculously short shorts.

While the four humans chatted away happily around the stove, Clack the chimp was in the meantime proving a big hit with the bunnies. He'd jumped off Mr Corncrake's lap and had swung over to them. He was like a bunny magnet. The chimpanzee attracted the rabbits like cheese is supposed to attract mice or marmalade attracts wasps, or how just about anything stealable attracts Grabby Hanson, our chief of police.

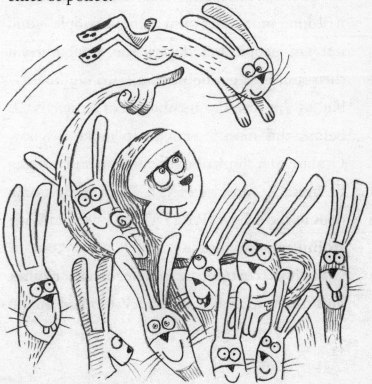

They were twitching the little pink bunny noses around the chimp. They were bobbing their bob tails, they were chattering their pairs of sticky-out front teeth, and they all seemed to be giving him their undivided attention.

Jilly was watching them with interest when there was a knock at the shack door. A moment later, Tie-Pin Petty-Mandrake's father, Wide Brim Petty-Mandrake, was standing in the room with them. Wide Brim is a VERY irritating man. I get on with most people – and not just people but *children* too, sometimes, if they stand far enough away from my beard – but, as I'm sure I've mentioned at least ONCE before, this man is enough to make a fellow Grubtowner think about selling up and moving to Werty . . . and we HATE Werty, so that only goes to show how IRRITATING we find Wide Brim Petty-Mandrake.

He was carrying a bundle of dry clothes, and trying to shake off a buck-toothed bunny who was clinging to the bottom of his trouser leg. 'Go and put these on at once,' he said, handing the clothes to Tie-Pin who was now toasty-warm in the borrowed blanket. 'No one in their right mind would leave a nearby lake unattended in the dark. It was a miracle you weren't all drowned!'

Wide Brim Petty-Mandrake is almost as good-looking as Grabby Hanson, who is SO handsome that he's better looking than most Hollywood movie stars who are just *pretending* to be policemen in their films. The trouble is, Petty-Mandrake has such a whining voice that you want to grab the nearest thing to muffle it: a pillow, a sheep, a passing cloud . . . And, not only that, he whinges, which means you're listening to someone whingeing in a whining voice, which certainly isn't a winning combination.

I heard a story – from Camshaft Thrift in THE RUSTY DOLPHIN, I think it was – that once, when Wide Brim Petty-Mandrake was amongst those people rescued by the lifeboat crew over at Limp (when the pleasure cruiser *The Doomed Sieve* suddenly sprang a surprise leak), they took him OUT of the lifeboat and put him back on the sinking cruiser 'for the safety of the other rescued passengers'. Apparently, so many of the people aboard the lifeboat had requested that *they* be put back in the sinking ship or in the sea rather than having to spend another MINUTE with that complaining, complaining, COMPLAINING man, the crew took the decision to put him back and come back for him – alone – later on. THAT'S how annoying most of us find him, and I'm sure you would too.

Now, can we *please* get on?

Good. Thank you. Wide-Brim Petty Mandrake led his son, Jilly and Mango from Rumpus Corncrake's shack, lighting the way ahead with a lamp he had attached to the front of that strange hat he always wears. Mango Claptrap reckoned it was an old bicycle lamp, but it certainly seemed to do the trick.

'What about the chimpanzee?' Jilly Cheeter asked the Sun-Ripe Raisin man in his open doorway.

'I'm here to take the children home,' Petty-Mandrake whined. 'Nobody said anything about a chimpanzee.'

'But we can't leave him here!' Jilly Cheeter protested.

'I can and I will!' said Wide Brim Petty-Mandrake. Tie-Pin was about to point out to his father that Mr Corncrake had saved him from drowning and that the chimpanzee was *their* responsibility, and that it was unfair to dump him on Mr Corncrake, when the Sun-Ripe Raisin man spoke for himself.

'I'm perfectly happy for the chimpanzee to stay the night,' he said. 'One of you could take him back to the old folks' home for me tomorrow.'

'I'd be glad to!' said Tie-Pin.

'Come on now, everyone!' said his father. 'Before we all catch our death of cold.'

Jilly Cheeter, Mango Claptrap and Tie-Pin Petty-Mandrake traipsed off through the darkness, past Rumpus Corncrake's vast vegetable patch – which seemed to have been stripped bare of just about every vegetable – following the light from Wide-Brim's hat-strapped lamp.

'Thanks again!' Tie-Pin called out to Rumpus Corncrake.

'Thank you for the hot chocolate!' Jilly Cheeter added.

'And the bubble wrap,' said Mango Claptrap.

'Take care!' the Sun-Ripe Raisin man called out as he went back inside and shut the door behind him. He was now not only sharing his home with a bunch of white bunnies but with a chattering chimp as well.

Chapter Five
Book 'em!

The next morning, after a late breakfast at the Claptrap house (whilst Tie-Pin returned to Corncrake's to take the chimp back to the old folks' home), Jilly Cheeter and Mango Claptrap headed down to the library to use the library computer. (There's only one.) They wanted to find out more about the habits of rabbits to try to make sense of why there suddenly seemed to be so many of them in and around town.

Grubtown Town Library wasn't a very impressive building back then. Quite the opposite, in fact. Three of its four walls were made of plywood, and the roof was made of corrugated iron. In all the time I'd known it, the corrugated iron was rusty, so the roof had rather a nice reddy brown look to it.

The library had been put up – 'built' is too grand a word to describe the putting-it-together process – nearer to a beach than a library should be. This meant that the books ended up a little damper (with more wrinkled pages) than was ideal. (Once Jilly Cheeter found a sea snail in a book about knots, and the photocopier was forever breaking down because it had sand in the mechanism.) But, as Mayor Flabby Gomez was always keen to point out, over in Werty they didn't even *have* a library.

Mrs Awning was using the computer when the pair arrived. She was sending an e-mail to the company that had made her bathroom cabinet. It was an e-mail of complaint. Earlier that morning, the cabinet had fallen off the bathroom wall above her basin and had hit her over her head just as she was about to brush her teeth. Not only had the blow to the head been painful in itself but it had also made her squirt the entire contents of a tube of toothpaste in her face. The 'whites' of her eyes were still bright red as she typed away, angrily jabbing at the K E Y B O A R D.

She'd needed a sticky plaster to put over the cut on her forehead, but her first-aid box had been in the fallen cabinet. In picking up the cabinet to reach the plasters, she'd cut herself on a piece of broken glass from one of its mirror-doors, so had dropped the cabinet.

On her foot.

That explained the additional plasters on her fingers. And the walking stick propped up against the computer table.

While they were waiting, Jilly Cheeter and Mango Claptrap went to look at the duck display that the librarian, Tamsin Thwack, was putting together. There were tables and shelves of brand-new books about ducks, along with some photos of local ducks, duck-related items and people. And then there was the three-metre-tall brightly painted papier-mâché model of a duck which Ms Thwack was moving into position.

'Need a hand, Ms Thwack?' asked Mango Claptrap, causing her to jump.

'Wooooah!' she said. 'I didn't see you there, Mango. No, I'm fine, thanks.'

'Nice duck, Ms Thwack,' said Jilly, looking up at its beautifully painted bill (which is the correct term for a duck's beak).

'Hello, Jilly,' said the librarian. 'There's a photograph of you in the display somewhere from back when you were town duck-gatherer—'

'Yerch!' said a unison of voices, rather rudely.

They turned to see a cluster of Foxes: Garrideb Fox and two of her brothers, Shaun and Fastbuck, each with a finger in their throat, as though trying to make themselves sick. The Foxes are Grubtown's family of duck-haters. Every town has one, but they're more noticeable in Grubtown because:

(a) we have so many ducks.
(b) we love our ducks more than most.

They particularly hate Jilly Cheeter because she gets on so well with ducks and they particularly hate Mango Claptrap because he gets on so well with Jilly Cheeter. That and the fact that Jilly and Mango keep doing heroic stuff and end up being awarded medals by the mayor, whilst they do bad stuff and end up being arrested rather a lot.

The last thing any of the Foxes would want to find in their local library was a DUCK display!

'Do I need to remind you that you three are banned from the library?' asked chief librarian, Tamsin Thwack.

'You can't ban us!' said Garrideb,

doing her pouty face.

'I can and I have. You can't go writing
rude words in all the library's duck books
and expect to be allowed back in here!'
said Tamsin Thwack. 'We had to go out
and buy all these new ones.'

'How do you know it was us?'

demanded a defiant Fastbuck.

'Because the books were issued to you.'

'Someone could have stolen them from us.'

'The rude words were in your handwriting.'

'Someone could have copied our handwriting.'

'You signed your insults.'

'Our signatures could have been forged.'

'The ink was traced back to your three pens.'

'Someone could have borrowed them.'

'Your fingerprints were found on each of the damaged books.'

'Just because we handled them, doesn't mean we wrote in them.'

'You videoed yourself defacing the books and posted the films on YouTube.'

'That could have been trick photography!'

'Traces of your DNA were found in the bite marks where you chewed several of the covers,' said Tamsin Thwack.

'Er . . . Er . . . we were hungry,' said Garrideb, rather feebly. She tried to flatten some nonexistent creases in her dress.

'And all three of you admitted it at the time,' said Ms Thwack.

'We could have been lying,' said Fastbuck.

'Yes!' said Shaun Fox. 'We're terrible liars . . .'

'So it seems,' said the librarian. 'Now get out of my library!'

Shaun muttered what might have been a rude word but he probably wasn't quite brave enough to say it properly or loud enough. As you can see from Jim's picture of her – which is a very good likeness – Tamsin Thwack isn't one of those storybook librarians with grey hair in a bun or half-moon glasses. Yes, she wears glasses, but they're lozenge-shaped, and her shiny black hair is cut into quite a trendy bob. You'll also have noticed that she's wearing a karate suit with a fancy logo on it. That fancy logo is for the **GRUBTOWN AND DISTRICT KARATE, KICK-BOXING AND ORIGAMI CLUB**, of which Ms Thwack is president. She can karate-chop bricks in two, kick down your front door if you've locked yourself out and left stuff cooking on the stove – I speak from experience here – and can make paper frogs that really jump . . . so, to put it another way, Ms Tamsin Thwack is NOT the kind of librarian you mess with.

Shaun, Fastbuck and Garrideb Fox sloped off like sulking teenagers, defiantly bumping into the nearest thing just to show that they were still being just-a-little-bit defiant. That 'nearest thing' was Mrs Awning who'd sent her e-mail and was now heading off for a hospital appointment. She slipped on the lino-tiled floor and twisted her ankle. Seeing what they'd done, the Foxes broke into a run and were out of the library in a flash.

While Tamsin Thwack went to get Dr Fraud from the reference section – being a fake doctor he likes to read medical books and journals so that he can appear to know what he's was talking about during medical emergencies – and while two library assistants helped Mrs Awning to her feet, Mango and Jilly went over to the computer table.

They found Hobo Browne placing a pair of wet underpants on the back of the old-fashioned computer monitor. 'It's good for drying them,' he told the children. 'That machine gets good and hot once it's been on a while.'

'And probably even hotter than usual with your underwear blocking off the air vents,' said Mango Claptrap, clearly impressed. Hobo Browne is homeless. He's what some people call a tramp. He likes to wash all his clothes once in a while (which he usually does by having a fully-clothed swim in the sea) but he likes a clean pair of undies more often than that. It's amazing where his drying vests and pants turn up around Grubtown. But I don't really want to talk about that. Ever.

'What are you two up to?' asked Hobo Browne, what with Jilly and Mango being local celebrities. Okay, they're not celebrities in the sense that Tawdry Hipbone the Grubtown-born movie star is, or Hybrid Byword the world's most famous (once dead) TV chef is, or even Purple Outing of **PURPLE OUTING'S MUSIC SHACK** is (and he's really just famous for being famous and extraordinarily rich). They're probably not even as famous as

Rumpus Corncrake who isn't really famous in his own right but IS famous as the Sun-Ripe Raisin man. But Jilly and Mango *are* very well-known for all they've done for Grubtown, and not just in Grubtown thanks to a certain Beardy Ardagh and his **GRuBtoWN taLes**. (Do you hear that honking sound? That's me blowing my own trumpet.)

'We're trying to find out more about rabbits,' Jilly Cheeter told Hobo Browne, pulling up a free chair next to Mango, who was already sitting in front of the computer.

'The plague, you mean?' said Hobo Browne.

'I thought it was supposed to be rats that carried the plague?' said Jilly.

'You mean rats that carried the fleas that carried the plague,' said Mango Claptrap.

'Rats?' said Hobo Browne. 'I thought you were talking about the plague of white bunnies that are talking over the town.'

'Well, they do seem to be spreading, Mr

Browne,' said Mango Claptrap, 'but don't you think "taking over the town" is a bit of an exaggeration?'

'You've obviously not seen today's paper, then!' said Hobo Browne. He pulled a crumpled copy out from under his shirt.

Jilly read the headline and gasped.

Chapter Six
The plague

Jilly Cheeter blinked, then read the headline of *The Grubtown Daily Herald* a second time.

MAYOR'S KNITTED
RESIDENCE ATTACKED
AND EATEN BY BUNNIES

'Blimey!' said Mango.

'Woweee!' she said, taking the newspaper from Hobo Browne and quickly reading the news report.

'No one was hurt,' said Browne.

'Apparently the mayor and mayoress were at the town hall watching Tundra in a pie-eating competition.' Tundra Gomez is Flabby and Pritt Gomez's only son.

'But what about the house?' said Mango Claptrap. 'Mayor Gomez loves that house. He spent forever knitting it!'

'Forever' is an exaggeration, but it did take years. The headline turned out to be an exaggeration too or, if not exactly an exaggeration, a little misleading. Yes, the rabbits had managed to take big bites out of a number of walls, doors, floors and ceilings before they were 'repelled' – that was the word *The Grubtown Daily Herald* used to describe the Gomezes' action – but most of the house was fine. (Well, as fine as a knitted house can be after a bunny attack.)

'This is CRAZY!' said Mango Claptrap when he'd finished reading the article. 'Where have all these bunnies come from?'

'And why are they behaving [...]
Jilly Cheeter. 'I thought rabbits w[...]
to be all fluffy and cute.'

'I've heard every kind of rumour,' [...]
Browne, flipping his underpants over [...] warm
on the other side, 'but I know what I know.'

'Tell us more,' said Jilly.

'Yes,' said Mango Claptrap excitedly. 'What
do you know?'

'Are you familiar with the row of abandoned
shops on Himble Street?'

'Of course we are!' said Jilly Cheeter. 'That's
where Farflung Heaps opened his pasta-and-
crispy-lettuce bar in the old Molten Lusty's
Discount Carpet Warehouse . . . for less than a
day!'

Hobo Browne shuddered at the memory of
the time much of Grubtown was covered in pasta
and tomato sauce. 'Well, I sometimes sleep in the
old shoe shop there when the weather turns cold
and keep some of my things there.'

...ings?' asked Jilly.

'My newspapers,* my bottle tops. Stuff like that,' said Hobo Browne. 'The other day, I was coming out of the old shoe shop when I heard a cry and went to investigate.'

'What kind of cry was it?' asked Mango Claptrap, eagerly leaning forward.

'A very strange cry,' said Hobo. 'It was such an unfamiliar sound, which is why I wanted to find out what had made it –' He stuffed a hand into the pocket of his coat and pulled out a big red hanky with white spots. He gave his nose a trumpet-like blow then stuffed it away again. 'I saw something disappearing into what was once Rapid Treacle's Magic Emporium. It used to be Herman's Socks and Ties before that.'

'Rapid Treacle?' said Jilly Cheeter. 'Wasn't he the magician who made himself disappear and hasn't been seen since?'

'That's the one.' Hobo nodded. 'About three years ago, he was doing a charity performance for

*The Grubtown Daily Herald and
The Grubtown Weekly Gerald

one of Shoona Loose's charities at the Town Hall.'
(It was for florists who suffered from hay fever, in
fact. They were raising money for hankies.)

'My dad was there when it happened!' said
Mango Claptrap. 'He said that Rapid Treacle
climbed into his magic cabinet and shut the door.
When his assistant opened it, he was gone. When
she closed it and opened it again, he was *still*
gone. After twenty minutes of waiting for him to
reappear, the audience gave up and went home.'
(Flabby Gomez had stayed behind to finish the
free crisps and orange squash.)

'And Treacle's Magic Emporium has been
empty ever since,' said Hobo Browne.

'And that was where the noise was coming
from?' said Jilly Cheeter.

Hobo Browne nodded. 'Through a gap in one
of the boarded-up windows, I saw more white
bunnies than I've ever seen in my entire life up.
They appeared to be arguing over a lettuce, or
whatever it was that's growing out of the walls.

That many bunnies must need a *lot* of food.'

'We were at the Sun-Ripe Raisin man's house last night,' said Jilly Cheeter, 'and his house was full of bunnies.'

'I'll bet it wasn't as full as the old Magic Emporium,' said Hobo.

'Shall we go and take a look?' said Mango Claptrap excitedly. 'It'd be great if we could solve the mystery of where all these bunnies are coming from.'

'Great idea,' said Jilly Cheeter.

They decided to walk to Himble Street. They weren't in a hurry, and it was a beautiful sunny day. They cut across the town square, passing Grabby Hanson running out of **OFFAL'S**

SUNBEDS, trying to hide the cash register under his policeman's jacket. He saw Jilly and Mango, but said nothing and kept on running.

About ten minutes later, a police car drove by with Officer Mustard Tripwire at the wheel. Grabby Hanson was in the back. He wound down his window and called Jilly and Mango over. 'Hi,' he said.

'Hello, Chief,' they said.

'Did you see anyone acting suspiciously outside Offal's Sunbeds a little while back?' he asked. 'About ten or fifteen minutes ago?'

'Just you, Chief,' said Mango Claptrap.

'With a cash register stuffed up the front of your police uniform,' Jilly added.

'And you'd be willing to testify to that in a court of law?'

'Sure we would,' said Mango Claptrap, with a solemn nod.

'Excellent,' said Grabby Hanson. 'Good work, kids. Thanks.' The Chief leant forward and tapped Mustard Tripwire on the shoulder. 'I'm placing myself under arrest on suspicion of theft from **OFFAL'S SUNBEDS**. We'd better take me down to the station for questioning.'

Mango and Jilly caught the words, 'Okay, Chief,' before the window was wound up again and the police car did a U-turn – narrowly avoiding a **NO U-TURNS** sign, and sped off back the way it had come.

Mango Claptrap and Jilly Cheeter admired the Chief's honesty. Most of us in Grubtown do. We've heard tales of some mightily corrupt officers in other places, but not here in Grubtown. Our chief is as quick to arrest himself as he would any other criminal. There are no 'favourites' around here. (Please excuse me while I wipe a tear of pride from the corner of my eye.)

Himble Street was even more dingy than Jilly Cheeter and Mango Claptrap had remembered. There were one or two shops still open amongst the mess, but the burnt-out wreck of a candle store and a fallen-down builders' merchants means that most people steer well clear of the area when shopping. Even the litter looks grubbier than in other parts of town, and the stray cats more scrawny and down-on-their-luck. The ducks in the flooded basements look that much more streetwise.

The sign to *Rapid Treacle's Magic Emporium*

still hung above the boarded-up windows, with its logo of a white-gloved hand pulling a rabbit out of a magician's hat. It was old and faded and splodged with dried tomato sauce. Someone had fly-posted across the boards, advertising the week of GRUNTING HedgePIGs

gigs over which someone else had sprayed some graffiti. The graffiti read: KILL ALL DUKCS with the word DUKCS crossed out with a line and DUCKS written next to it.

'Looks like some of those Foxes have been here,' said Jilly.

'And not that long ago,' said Mango Claptrap.

Jilly Cheeter touched the spray paint with the tip of her finger. It was dry. 'What makes you say that?' she asked.

Mango Claptrap pointed at the GRUNTING HedgePIGs posters, all pasted up in a row. 'They say "ALL THIS WEEK AT THE LIMP AUDITORIUM" and the concerts were only last week –'

'And the graffiti has been sprayed over them, so it must have been done more recently!' Jilly Cheeter grinned.

'Exactly!' said Mango.

Now Jilly tried the door – it was open a crack – but then hesitated. She felt they were being watched. She saw a single pair of rabbit's eyes staring at her from the broken window of another abandoned shop, just a hop away. Turning back to the door, she pushed it wide – on creaking hinges – and she and Mango Claptrap entered the emporium.

Neither Mango nor Jilly had been quite sure what to expect. Maybe the bunnies would be long gone, leaving nothing more than bunny balls – that's a polite phrase for rabbit poo – and a few white hairs, or maybe they'd still be there.

They were still there all right, but – even though Hobo Browne had said that there'd been plenty of them – there were far, far more than they'd expected. It was more crowded than a special Grubtown Town Hall town meeting (which is almost as crowded as an abandoned magic emporium packed with white rabbits). There were rabbits EVERYWHERE.

'Wow!' said Jilly Cheeter.

'Wow!' said Mango Claptrap. There was no way that they could get in with all those bunnies in there. 'Let's try round the back.'

They slipped down an alleyway, covered in more DUKCS graffiti and came out at the back of the row of abandoned shops. 'Now all we have to do is work out which is the back of the Magic Emporium,' said Mango.

'Any bright ideas?' asked Jilly Cheeter.

'Not really,' said Mango.

'How about this one?' said Jilly when they'd walked about halfway down. 'The window frames are painted the same colour as the ones at the front of the store.'

'Genius!' Mango grinned.

Chapter Seven
Bunny Trouble!

The back room of **Rapid Treacle's Magic Emporium** was a bit of a puzzle to Jilly Cheeter and Mango Claptrap. The puzzly bit of a puzzle. Not the picture on the box, or the warning about the small parts being a choking hazard. It was quite a small room, with a battered old desk and chair and a (closed) door obviously leading into the main part of the shop.

What made it unusual — quite apart from being completely and utterly bunny-free — was the large bendy tube (thick enough for a child to crawl through) which came up out of the middle of the floor, arched across the room and disappeared through a hole in the wall to the front.

Mango Claptrap bent down to take a closer look. So did Jilly Cheeter. They squished it. They woggled it. They walked around it. What was it? What did it do? What was it for?

'It must come out behind the shop counter, the other side of the wall,' said Mango.

'Or *under* the counter,' said Jilly Cheeter. An idea had just formed in her mind.

'Why under?' asked Mango Claptrap.

'What's the shop's logo?' she asked.

Mango Claptrap thought of the sign hanging outside the front of *Rapid Treacle's Magic Emporium*. 'A hand in a white glove pulling a rabbit out of a magician's top hat, by its ears,' he said.

'And how's that trick done?'

Mango shrugged. 'With a false bottom in the hat, with the rabbit hiding inside, or . . . ' His face broke into a smile.

'Or the bottom of the hat somehow opens, and the magician can reach into the hat through to a secret compartment below!' said Jilly Cheeter.

'Aha!' said Mango Claptrap, and it was

amazing just how much excitement he could pack into those three little letters. (Go on. Count them. Just an 'A' and an 'h' and an 'a'.) 'You think Rapid Treacle demonstrated magic tricks in the shop, and that he had a kind of secret tunnel leading from the basement to under the counter . . . to under his *hat*?'

'Exactly!' said Jilly. 'But not a tunnel for people but for –'

'White rabbits!' said Mango Claptrap. He whooped with delight.

'I wonder if that means that there's a basement full of bunnies down below?' said Jilly. 'Or whether they all hopped out long ago?' She tapped the wooden floorboards with her foot.

Mango was thinking. He reached inside a pocket of his ridiculously short shorts and pulled out a tiny spiral-bound notebook and a stubby pencil. He then sat on the old desk with his feet on the chair, using his lap to rest the book on. He started to jot down numbers.

'Let's say that a mummy rabbit has ten baby rabbits a year from three litters, each with two babies one male and one female . . .' he sucked his pencil . . . 'and one litter with four babies, two male and two female . . .' he did some more frantic scribbling.

Jilly Cheeter looked to see what he was writing. It looked like gobbledygook to her:

$$x = ((n/2)*2) = n \text{ (for 2 offspring litters)}$$
and
$$x = ((n/2)*4) \text{ for 4 offspring litter.}$$

'Huh?' she said (which is probably what I would have done).

'Where "n" is the answer to previous formulae,' said Mango Claptrap, as though that explained everything. (Jilly was beginning to wonder whether he was spending too much time with Informative Boothe, Grubtown's resident know-all who'd been teaching him rather a lot lately.)

'So how many bunnies would that mean in three years?' she asked. Jilly was thinking of the three years since Rapid Treacle had stepped into his magic disappearing cabinet, never to be seen again. What if there'd been some bunnies down in his secret basement, waiting for him to return, but he never had?

Mango had pulled his shoes and socks off and was now counting with his toes. 'How many? Er . . . about fifty-five thousand, two hundred and ninety-six,' he said.

'Fifty-five thousand, two hundred and ninety-six bunnies starting with just two bunnies three years ago?'

Mango nodded. 'And a mummy bunny probably has MORE than ten baby bunnies a year, so we're talking –'

'Thousands and thousands and thousands of bunnies!' said Jilly Cheeter. 'No wonder Grubtown is suffering a plague of rabbits!' She felt a warm glow of pride that she and Mango had been the ones to solve the reason why there was a plague (even if Mango had done all the actual maths on his own).

'We need to find a way down into the basement,' said Jilly Cheeter, 'just to be sure that there aren't any that can't find their way out.'

'Just let me get my shoes back on!' said Mango Claptrap, who was struggling into his socks. Soon the two friends were hunting for a trapdoor – for any kind of door – but couldn't find one anywhere.

'There must be a way down to the basement from the front of the shop,' said Mango Claptrap. 'But there's no way we can get in there.'

'We'll have to come back,' said Jilly, 'but we'll need to see the mayor first, and tell him about our discovery. We're going to have to try to find homes for an awful lot of bunnies!'

Jilly and Mango found Grubtown's mayor,

Flabby Gomez, at **MINTY'S CAKE SHOP** where he was being photographed sampling a new cake named after him. 'The Flabby' looked like a bright pink three-tiered wedding cake but

flabbier, as though it was made of something much wobblier than usual. Minty Glibb had baked it in honour of the mayor to mark his first full year in the official mayoral (knitted) residence. He wasn't going to let the small matter of his house being nibbled by bunnies put him off the opportunity of eating FREE CAKE. (The mayor and I were once trapped in Minty Glibb's shop overnight and had to eat the unsold cakes and pastries in order to survive, so I can confirm that she's a *very* good baker.)

Mayor Gomez had just finished a speech (with his mouth full) and photographs had been taken of the empty plate and a few crumbs – he hadn't been able to resist – when Jilly Cheeter and Mango Claptrap arrived.

'Excuse me, Mister Mayor,' said Jilly Cheeter, 'but we think we've found out where the bunnies are coming from who attacked your house.'

She and Mango proceeded to explain everything. Flabby Gomez listened in amazed silence, eating his way through:

    three chocolate éclairs
    four blueberry muffins
    two iced buns
    two cardboard cupcakes
    one Eccles cake
    five millionaire's slices
    and two Bakewell tarts

He didn't notice that the two cupcakes were made of cardboard (as part of a window display) because he was so engrossed in what the children were telling him.

'Amazing!' he said, when they'd finished. (Actually, he did a big burp followed by a 'Pardon me!' and *then* said, 'Amazing!') 'I'll get someone over to the old Magic Emporium as soon as possible, to make sure there are no trapped rabbits. Then we're going to have to find a way of gathering them all up.'

Just then, Police Chief Grabby Hanson arrived at Flabby Gomez's side. 'Mister Mayor!' he said. 'Reports are coming in that the Grubtown Library has been destroyed during the librarians' lunch hour!'

Jilly Cheeter gasped.

Mango Claptrap gasped.

'Any suspects?' asked the mayor.

'Tamsin Thwack has her suspicions,' said the Police Chief.

Jilly Cheeter and Mango Claptrap immediately thought of the big duck display.

'The Fox family?' they asked, as one.

Chapter Eight
Big discoveries

What with the brand-new duck display in the middle of the library, and the trouble Tamsin Thwack had had with Garrideb, Shaun and Mantle Fox earlier that day, you can see why the chief librarian immediately suspected that it was the duck-hating Foxes who'd turned the library into pile of rubble.

Jilly Cheeter and Mango Claptrap weren't so sure.

'Knocking a building down is a bit much, even for them!' said Jilly.

'A loud sneeze could probably have

knocked that place down,' Mango pointed out. 'It's only plywood walls and a tin roof. But still …'

As it turned out, it didn't take long for Grabby Hanson to uncover the truth. (I've said it before and I'll say it again: he's a splendid chief of police.) There had been no witnesses to the attack because, back then, the library closed for lunch every day, and every day Tamsin Thwack drove her staff in the library minibus (and mobile dog grooming parlour) to THE RUSTY DOLPHIN CAFE for a light lunch. But while he was picking through the wreckage of the scene of the crime, he noticed something attached to a telegraph pole on the opposite side of the road. It glinted in the sunlight.

He wandered over to investigate. It was a CCTV camera and there appeared to be a phone number printed on the side. Grabby Hanson shinned up the pole and, holding on tight with his knees, managed to take his mobile phone out of his pocket and to punch in the number.

The phone rang three times at the other end as he climbed back down, and then was answered by Farflung Heaps, marine biologist and head of our local Angry Mob. 'Yes?' he said.

The Chief recognised his voice at once. 'Heaps? This is Chief Hanson,' he said, brushing the knees of his trousers with his free hand. 'You've got a camera pointing at the library. Why?'

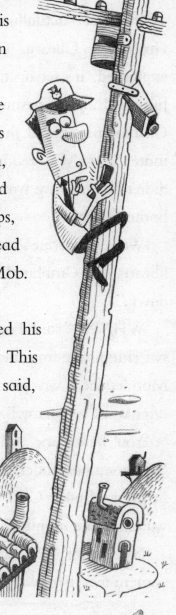

'It's not actually pointing directly at Grubtown Library, Chief,' Farflung Heaps explained. 'It's set up there to keep an eye on Jip and Binkey's nesting site.' Jip the pelican is Grubtown's official mascot and Binkey is his mate. 'They've already had one egg which didn't hatch so we want to make sure no one's bothering them.'

'Well, someone's seriously bothered the library,' said Grabby Hanson. 'It's been knocked down.'

'WHAT?!?' said Farflung Heaps, his voice switching tone from marine biologist to Angry Mob leader. 'I was planning to get a book out after work tomorrow!'

'You heard me,' said the Chief of Police. 'Someone has knocked the library down right in front of your CCTV camera. Isn't anyone watching the monitor?'

'No, Chief. We simply record what the camera sees then play it back if we want to find out what's happened during the day.'

'Well, I certainly want to find out who did what to the library,' said Chief Grabby Hanson. 'Can you fix that for me?'

'Sure, Chief,' said Farflung Heaps. 'I'll set it up for you right away. How soon can you get to me?'

'Where are you?' asked Grabby Hanson. He was back amongst the library wreckage now. He'd found a box of free library bookmarks and was busy stuffing his pockets full of them.

'In my new offices at the Grubtown Aquarium and Carwash,' said Farflung Heaps.

Chief Hanson looked at his watch. 'I'll be there in ten minutes,' he said.

When Farflung Heaps played the recording to the policeman, it didn't show the Fox family attacking the library.

No.

Jilly Cheeter and Mango Claptrap were right. The Fox family may be bad, but not bad in a knocking-down-a-library kind of way.

In fact, no humans had been responsible for such an act. Neither were the Grubtown rats, of course.

The CCTV footage showed that − you guessed it − it was a horde of passing bunnies who'd done the dirty deed (or a 'marauding gang of bunnies' as one of the local papers* put it).

*The Grubtown Daily Herald and
The Grubtown Weekly Gerald

Somehow, the library-trashing bunny clip soon ended up on YouTube and has become a firm favourite with the Fox family, who particularly love the part where a bunch of bunnies, led by a big buck rabbit, drag Tamsin Thwack's papier-mâché duck outside and break it to pieces.

For the weeks that followed the events in this **GRuBtoWN TaLe**, Derek and Bunty Fox and their children watched the clip again and again. Two of the boys – Mantle and Fastbuck – went around wearing T-shirts with **THEM RABBITS HAD THE RIGHT** written on Mantle's and **IDEA, YEAH!** on Fastbuck's. (There was even a rumour that the Foxes built an effigy of one of the rabbits and worshipped it as a duck-hating god, but Bunty Fox has always denied this.)

With confirmation from Informative Boothe that Mango Claptrap's calculations about the ever-increasing number of bunnies were spot-on, and with a trail of destruction which now included the mayor's knitted residence, the library and numerous gardens (including Rumpus Corncrake's beloved vegetable patch, of course), the need to tackle the bunnies was now Grubtown's Official Number One Problem To Be Solved.

Flabby Gomez declared a state of emergency, which involved all three members of the local police force wearing red armbands, his having to wear a special state-of-emergency hat, and calling an emergency special state-of-emergency meeting at the town hall for 4.00 p.m. that day.

Although, as a citizen of Grubtown, I was at the meeting – I had to be – I won't waste your time or mine telling you all about it because, like most special meetings at Grubtown Town Hall, there was rather a lot of talking and not much got done.

Jilly Cheeter and Mango Claptrap – who'd been officially sworn in as members of the Special Bunny Task Force, and now also wore red armbands – had noticed that Rumpus Corncrake hadn't been at the meeting, so decided to check that he was okay.

When they arrived at his shack, which looked very different in daylight, they were greeted by the extraordinary sight of Clack the chimpanzee prancing around the outside of the house being followed by a winding column of white rabbits. The retired Sun-Ripe Raisin man was sitting on an upturned bucket, tapping out time with his raisin-headed silver-topped cane. He stood up when he saw the children.

'Hi, Mr Corncrake!' said Mango Claptrap.

'Hello,' said Rumpus Corncrake, a large smile spreading across his oh-so-wrinkly-raisin-like face.

'Didn't Tie-Pin come and collect Clack this morning, like he said he would?' asked Jilly Cheeter. 'And take him back to the old folks' home?'

'Indeed he did,' said Rumpus Corncrake, 'but for some strange reason, the chimp seems to have taken a shine to me, and he came straight back.'

'Funny that,' said Mango Claptrap, looking the Sun-Ripe Raisin man straight in the eye.

'Y-Yes,' said the man, a little hesitantly. 'Funny that.'

'It's amazing how the bunnies seem to like him so much,' said Jilly Cheeter, watching the chimp. 'They follow him like the rats in *The Pied*

Piper of Hamelin!' (Which, if you didn't know, is a story about a piper who can get rats – and, later, children – to follow him everywhere.)

'Amazing,' agreed Rumpus Corncrake.

'Mr Corncrake?' said Mango Claptrap.

'Yes, Mango?'

'When did you get the job as the Sun-Ripe Raisin man? Was it about three years ago?'

'Er, about then. Yes,' said Rumpus Corncrake. He sounded a little cautious.

'Have you ever had a pet ape?' asked Mango Claptrap.

Rumpus Corncrake looked taken aback. Jilly Cheeter look puzzled. What was Mango Claptrap on about now?

'It's just that you and Clack seem to get on so well that I was wondering whether you've ever owned a chimpanzee?'

'Well. I . . . er . . .'

'When we were at Rapid Treacle's Magic Emporium earlier today, I saw a poster on the wall, and it told me two very interesting things I didn't know about the magician,' Mango continued. 'Firstly, the picture showed him wearing a mask with question marks all over it – making him look all the more mysterious and magical – and, secondly, he had a chimpanzee next to him, dressed in clothes identical to his.'

The colour seemed to drain from Rumpus Corncrake's wrinkled face.

'Hang on! I get it!' said Jilly Cheeter (who got it). 'Didn't you tell us that, before you got the job as the Sun-Ripe Raisin man you spent years being anonymous on stage –'

'Because you don't really have "an actor's face", was what you said, Mr Corncrake,' Mango Claptrap added. 'Wasn't it?'

'And you couldn't really be much more anonymous than a magician hiding behind a mask!' said Jilly Cheeter. She turned to Mango. 'You're a genius!' she told him.

'Only if I'm right,' said Mango Claptrap.

Rumpus Corncrake sat back down on the upturned bucket with a thud. 'Oh, you're right,' he said. 'I'm Rapid Treacle . . . or I was. Who'd want to see someone with a face like mine on stage? I'd frighten everyone in the front row!'

'But your face was famous as the Sun–Ripe Raisin man!' Mango Claptrap protested. 'No one was afraid of it then.'

'That's because I was *supposed* to look as wrinkled as a dried and shrivelled grape. I was *supposed* to be as close to a raisin as a man could be without a silly costume! But as anything else? No way . . .'

'But what happened?' asked Jilly Cheeter. 'What made you abandon your magic act, your chimp and those poor rabbits?'

'Sniffles and Snuffles? I didn't abandon them. I took them with me!'

'They were your stage rabbits?'

He nodded.

'Then, how come your abandoned

emporium has turned into the world's biggest bunny factory?' asked Mango Claptrap, and he proceeded to tell Rapid Treacle/The Sun-Ripe Raisin man/Rumpus Corncrake what they'd found.

'But that's unbelievable! Terrible! Shocking!' said Corncrake when he'd finished. 'You mean that all these rabbits overrunning Grubtown are my fault? But it doesn't make any sense!'

'Perhaps Sniffles and Snuffles had had a few baby bunnies without you realising . . . ones you didn't know about,' said Jilly Cheeter, 'and they got left behind when you went –'

'And grew up to have bunnies of their own,' said Mango Claptrap.

Rumpus Corncrake's mouth hung open like a broken pedal bin. 'No!' he groaned.

'What made you decide to disappear for real, Mr Corncrake?' asked Mango Claptrap. 'Or should that be Mr Treacle?'

'No, it's Corncrake. I used the name Rapid Treacle as stage name when I hid my shame – my face – and became a masked magician. To start with, I loved being the centre of attention . . . the star of my own show. Then, as time went on, I got more and more depressed that I had all this recognition without daring to let anyone see me for who I really was. In the end, it became too much, so I decided to quit halfway through a show and slunk away into the night with my bunnies . . .' The Sun-Ripe Raisin man hung his head in shame. 'Only now it turns out that I left some behind. *What have I done?!*'

Chapter Nine
Bunny! Bunny! Bunny!

Now that Rumpus Corncrake realised that each and every one of these bunnies must be a direct descendant of his own beloved Sniffles and Snuffles – who had always pretended to be one and the same bunny in his magic act as Rapid Treacle – he wanted to do everything he could to help put things right.

The two biggest challenges for Grubtown's Special Bunny Task Force were: (1) How to get the bunnies to go where they wanted them to; and (2) where to put them all, especially if they were going to have MORE baby bunnies.

'The second part is easy,' said Rumpus Crake. 'The reason why I'm living in a shack on the outskirts of Grubtown is that I'm having a house built on Incredibly Nice Island.'

'But that's a private island,' said Jilly Cheeter. She'd seen photographs of it on posters of the coastline in the **GRUBTOWN TOURIST INFORMATION AND GARDEN WASTE RECYCLING CENTRE** (on the wall above the donkey dung bin).

'I know,' said Rumpus Corncrake. 'I own it. I bought it with all the money I made from my years of being the face of Sun-Ripe Raisins!'

'The bunnies would love having a whole island to themselves, and they wouldn't be able to swim all the way back here and cause more trouble!' said Mango Claptrap. 'Are you sure you wouldn't mind sharing it with thousands of bunnies?'

'Not at all!' beamed Corncrake. Mango wondered how long it would be before he'd have to share it with MILLIONS of bunnies, but didn't say anything.

'But how do we get them to the island?' said Jilly Cheeter.

'On the ships I've got delivering the building materials, I suppose,' said Rumpus Corncrake. 'They could take thousands of bunnies at a time.'

'I think what Jilly means, Mr Corncrake, is how do we catch them all in the first place?'

Jilly Cheeter had the answer. It was staring her in the face (literally) in the same way that it's sort-of staring YOU in the face (not literally): the chimpanzee, of course. He was standing directly in front of Jilly, Mango and Corncrake, with a rabbit under each arm and swarms of them around his feet.

'Clack!' she said. 'They'll follow Clack anywhere!'

'His name is Blump,' said Corncrake. 'Well, it *was* Blump before he was renamed Clack . . . Blump always loved Sniffles and Snuffles and they – and their bunny descendants – certainly seem to love him.'

'So we'll tell Mayor Gomez and Chief Hanson about the ships and the island, then you can get Clack – er – Blump to round up the bunnies and to follow him into cages in the backs of lorries or something!' said an excited Mango Claptrap. 'That sounds like a plan.'

It was not only a plan. It was also a very GOOD plan which is why, as I'm writing this, all the bunnies are now living on **INCREDIBLY NICE ISLAND** which has been renamed **INCREDIBLY NICE WITH RATHER A LOT OF BUNNIES ON IT ISLAND**. (Rumpus Corncrake had to pay to have it renamed, of course. As mayor, Flabby Gomez got rather a lot of money for that.) The island has become something of a tourist attraction and is very popular with day-trippers who want to see more bunnies than humanly imaginable, and to be photographed with the wonderfully

wrinkled one-time Sun-Ripe Raisin man.

Interestingly, Clack (formerly known as Blump) has chosen to stay living at **THE GRUBTOWN HOME FOR OLD FOLKS** because, I assume, he'd made so many friends there and is (you'll remember) in charge of the television remote control in the TV lounge.

It turned out that the final straw leading to the unhappy Rumpus Corncrake giving up being Rapid Treacle and fleeing partway through a magic show had been directly to do with Blump. It seems that the chimp had also had enough of their show. He'd done a disappearing act of his own, which was why Corncrake couldn't take him with him to start his new life. Two weeks before the show at the Town Hall where Rapid Treacle had magicked himself out of existence, Blump had packed his chimp-sized suitcase with chimp-sized clothes (matching Treacle's stage outfit) and left. No one knows where he went until he ended up by being bought by Asphalt Nosegay for the old folks' home that day.

Still, Blump and Corncrake are certainly glad to be back in touch today, and Blump spends most weekends on the island with the ex-magician and – it goes without saying – all those rabbits.

As for the library, Flabby Gomez has big plans for a new one. The mayor's (long dead) father, Big Man Gomez, hated books. He had one in which he kept a record of who owed him money, and where he wrote lots of notes about why he disliked certain people and what he'd like to do to them. But he never read books for pleasure. He said that books were for *girls*, somehow making this sound like a bad thing. Flabby Gomez, on the other hand, loves books. He has many thousands of his own in his own private library, mostly cookbooks (along with signed copies of many of mine, of course). He arranged for a mobile library to go around Grubtown until the new one was built.

THE GRUBTOWN MOBILE TOWN LIBRARY AND CHIP VAN proved a great success. It was stocked with brand-new books which, though they got a bit greasy and smelled of chip fat and vinegar, were far less damp, wrinkle-paged and sandy than those in the original library. So everything would have been fine if Werty hadn't gone and got a mobile library all of its own: a mobile library which was much, much, bigger. This was no van, it was a custom-built mobile library the size of a big lorry . . .

. . . and there was no way that Mayor Flabby Gomez was going to let those knuckle-heads over in Werty have a better mobile library than us. So **THE GRUBTOWN MOBILE TOWN LIBRARY AND CHIP VAN** turned back into a plain old chip van, and Mayor Gomez went out and bought the biggest, flashiest, bluest mobile library he could find. On the cheap.

This enormous mobile library was delivered on the back of an even bigger lorry, which should have been a clue about what was to follow. If you buy a truck, someone can drive that truck to you or you can drive it yourself. Why go to the trouble of putting that truck on the back of *another* one? The mayor's brother, Hacking-Cough Gomez soon found out why.

Once the new Grubtown Mobile Town Library was unloaded, had been signed for, and the delivery lorry had driven off, Hacking-Cough Gomez climbed aboard, started up the engine and drove straight off the road and into a beach hut, splintering it like matchwood.

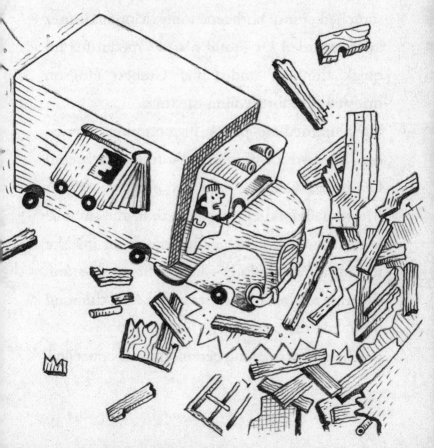

Hacking-Cough was shaken but unharmed.

The only injury was to Mrs Awning who'd been sitting in front of the beach hut, blowing up an inflatable beach toy shaped like a giant strawberry, when the accident occurred. She swallowed half of the inflatable soft fruit in the commotion and it had to be removed by Dr Fraud at the scene, using nothing but a hastily snatched pair of barbecue tongs. Mayor Gomez later awarded Dr Fraud a silver medal for his quick thinking and Chief Grabby Hanson arrested him for stealing the tongs.

An immediate police investigation, carried out by two of Grubtown's finest (Sergeant Constable Gelatine and his nephew Officer Mustard Tripwire) revealed that the mobile library had been in no fit state to be on the road in the first place – hence the crash – and was in even less of a fit state to be on the road following the crash.

The grand opening ceremony was cancelled,

the photographers and TV crew sent away, and the mayor instructed our two local papers* not to mention it, in case the people of Werty got wind of our misfortune.

And that's now the Grubtown Town Library: a huge no-longer-mobile mobile library truck half on the beach road and half on the beach itself, at a funny angle near Cripp's Corner.

Chief Librarian Tamsin Thwack and her library assistants did their best, loading it with greasy, vinegar-smelling books which soon became damp, crinkle-paged and sandy, too. They put colourful pictures on the walls, and there isn't a single SSHH! or SILENCE! or YOU'RE NOT HERE TO HAVE A GOOD TIME sign in sight.

As well as her **GRUBTOWN AND DISTRICT KARATE, KICK-BOXING AND ORIGAMI CLUB** karate suit, Tamsin Thwack now wears special-issue shoes with extra-grip-soles to try and stay as upright as possible when working

*The Grubtown Daily Herald and
The Grubtown Weekly Gerald

there on its oh-so-sloping floor.

By the entrance, just inside the door of the new library, there's a photograph of Tie-Pin Petty-Mandrake standing next to Jilly Cheeter and Mango Claptrap who are both proudly displaying their latest medals. In the background is what remains of the old library, a pile of plywood and corrugated iron. It acts as a permanent reminder of what happens when bunnies turn bad.

THE END

Another word from Beardy Ardagh

I f you'd like to write to me, that's fine. I may even ENJOY getting a letter from you. (Stranger things have happened.) But, if you're hoping for me to reply then PLEASE ENCLOSE A STAMPED, SELF-ADDRESSED ENVELOPE. In other words, write your *own* address on an envelope, stick a stamp on it, and enclose it with your letter in a *second* envelope stamped and addressed to:

Beardy Ardagh,
c/o Faber & Faber,
Bloomsbury House
74–77 Great Russell Street
London
WC1B 3DA

and write **GRuBtoWN taLes** in the bottom left-hand corner.

I can't PROMISE that I'll reply, I may be busy jelly-wrestling or try to teach my old beard new tricks, but you're FAR MORE LIKELY to get a reply than someone who expects me to spend all my money on postage stamps.

Now, please let me sleep.

(Just some of) the folk who pop up in GRuBtoWN taLes

Jilly Cheeter girl and one-time duck-gatherer

Mango Claptrap a short boy in short trousers, whatever the weather

Manual Org a smoothy skinned fellow

Flabby Gomez Mayor of Grubtown

Kumquat 'Grabby' Hanson the chief of police

The Grumbly girls the seven Grumbly daughters

Hacking-Cough Gomez the mayor's brother

Big Man Gomez the mayor's dead dad

Pritt Gomez the mayor's wife

Tundra Gomez the mayor's son and heir

Formal Dripping official village idiot for the nearby village of Werty

Derek,Bunty,Shaun,Mantle,Fastbuck & Garrideb Fox the duck-hating Fox family of humans (not foxes)

Rambo Sanskrit council job-giver-outer

Sonia Pipkin local builder

The troll inhabitant of Beardy Ardagh's airing cupboard

Mrs Awning town accident-waiting-to-happen, first name unknown

Minty Glibb owner of Minty's Cake Shop

Mickey 'Steamroller' Johnson doughnut-loving steamroller driver

Leggy Prune the future Mrs Johnson

Mrs Johnson the former Leggy Prune

Constable Gelatine a police sergeant

Mustard Tripwire an officer of the law and
Gelatine's nephew

Galaxy Tripwire a train driver and former
beauty queen

Relish Tripwire a tropical fish salesperson

Informative Boothe a very knowledgeable chap

Hobo Browne a gentleman of the road/smelly
tramp

Camshaft Thrift owner of The Rusty Dolphin
Cafe

Farflung Heaps self-appointed leader of an
angry mob

Garlic Hamper the lighthouse keeper

Shoona Loose the world-famous singer who
does a lot for animal charities

Tawdry Hipbone movie star

Snooks Miss Hipbone's pampered pooch

Luminous Shard bald heckler and mechanic

Carlo Monte the riverboat gambler

Lefty Scorn proprietor of Scorn's Laundrette
   & Jeweller's

Acrid Scorn an irresponsible dumper of
   hazardous waste

Jip the town pelican (official mascot)

Marley Gripe a painter of signs

Dr Fraud a pretend doctor (but he's cheap)

Sloop Cheeter Jilly's dad

Harvey the Cheeter family dog

Furl Claptrap Mango's dad

Carport Claptrap Mango's mum

Vestige Claptrap Mango's brother

Claws their cat

Partial Coggs Grubtown's resident artist

Slackjaw Gumshoe paint & hardware store owner

Purple Outing very rich owner of Purple Outing's Music Shack

Hind-Leg Outing amongst other things, mother of Purple's vast number of children

Wide Brim Petty-Mandrake a regular complainer

Tie-Pin Petty-Mandrake son of Wide Brim (poor kid)

Hetty Glue-Pen cinema manager and projectionist

Condo Blotch former cleaner now head of her very own keep-fit and health-food empire

Emily Blotch Condo's daughter

Free-Kick leader of the escaped lab rats

Lulu Free-Kick's mate for life

Rapid Treacle stage name of the one-time masked magician

Tamsin Thwack librarian, and president of the Grubtown and District Karate, Kick-Boxing and Origami Club

Glowering Silt general manager of Fettle's hotel

Avid Folklore manager of Fettle's hotel

Chevvy Offal owner of Offal's Sunbeds

Premix Stipend victim of one of Offal's sunbeds

Pageant Conquest food-maker (and Grabby Hanson's sister)

Rumpus Corncrake best known as being the wrinkly-faced Sun-Ripe Raisin man

Hybrid Byword the (once dead) TV chef

Limbo Goulash an office worker

Clam Wretching founder of Wretching's Dairy

Barton Wretching her son and current owner of the dairy

Beardy Ardagh honoured citizen of Grubtown and the teller of these tales

The delightful Beardy Ardagh tells of other GRuBtoWN taLes

If you want to grow up to be a healthy, happy person with LOTS OF FRIENDS, it is very important that you read all the **GRuBtoWN taLes**. Just to make sure that you've read each of those published so far – INCLUDING THIS ONE BY NOW – I've taken the time and trouble to tell you a bit about the others, over the next few pages. So CHECK THEM OUT.

Immediately.

Thank you.

Now leave me alone.

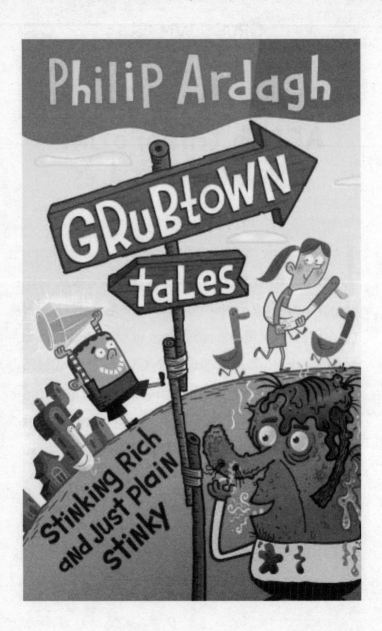

Philip Ardagh

GRuBtoWN taLes

Stinking Rich and Just Plain Stinky

GRuBtoWN taLes
Book One

StinkiNg Rich aNd
Just PlaiN StiNky

or

The Repulsive Mister Org

Grubtown is full of oddballs — from the singing Grumbly girls to a family of duck-haters, and an out-sized mayor who's knitting a new house — but Manual Org is too repulsive even for them. Getting him to leave town is top priority, until the discovery of a humongous diamond changes everything.

GRuBtoWN taLes
Book Two

The YeaR That It RaiNed Cows

or

That Well-Known Secret Door

A startled cow falling out of nowhere onto Limbo Goulash while he's riding Marley Gripe's bicycle marks the start of a chain of events strange even by Grubtown's standards. Soon damaged property includes **PURPLE OUTING'S MUSIC SHACK** and Minty Glibb's attempt at the world's largest (strawberry) jelly-trifle. With Mayor Flabby Gomez throwing a wobbly, all chief of police, Grabby Hanson, can do is have the cow-fearing townsfolk watch the skies. Underground, meanwhile, there lies another big surprise.

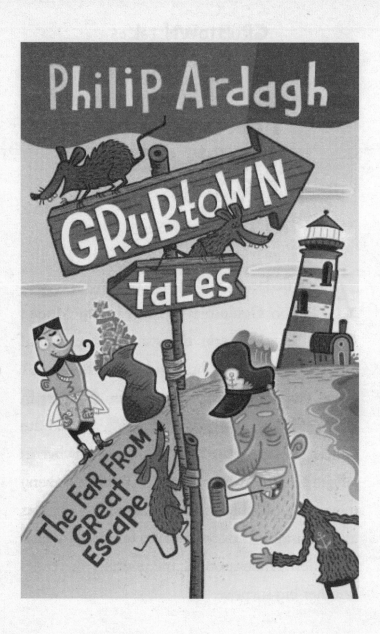

Philip Ardagh

GRuBtoWN
taLes

The FaR FRoM
GReat
EscaPe

GRuBtoWN taLes
Book Three

The FaR FRoM GReat EscaPe

or

The Light, the Switch and the Wardrobe

When the local lighthouse is plunged into darkness and a ship runs aground – flattening THE RUSTY DOLPHIN – it's hard to imagine things can get much worse in Grubtown. But then there's a jailbreak and the Police Department (all three of them) needs all the help it can get from the (often bonkers) townsfolk. No wonder more trouble is waiting just around the corner.

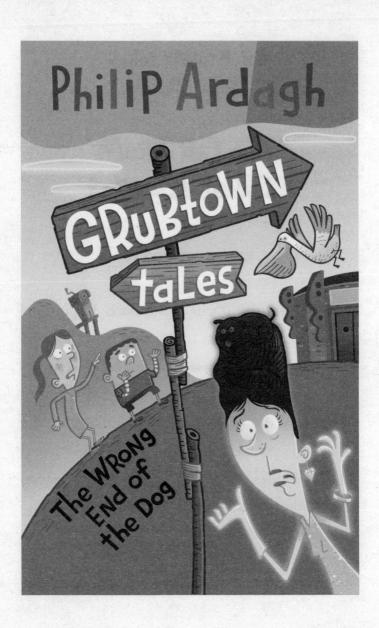

PhiliP Ardagh

GRuBtoWN taLes

The WRoNg End of the Dog

GRuBtoWN taLes
Book Four

The WRoNg ENd of the Dog

or

The Pedal-Bin Pelican

When famous film star Tawdry Hipbone visits Grubtown for the world premiere of her latest movie, *For the Love of Ducks II*, Mayor Flabby Gomez couldn't be more excited but, as usual, nothing goes to plan. Miss Hipbone's dog, Snooks, is snatched by a low-flying pelican, and it's a race against time to find him, in a rescue attempt involving Grubtown's usual ragbag of bungling buffoons.

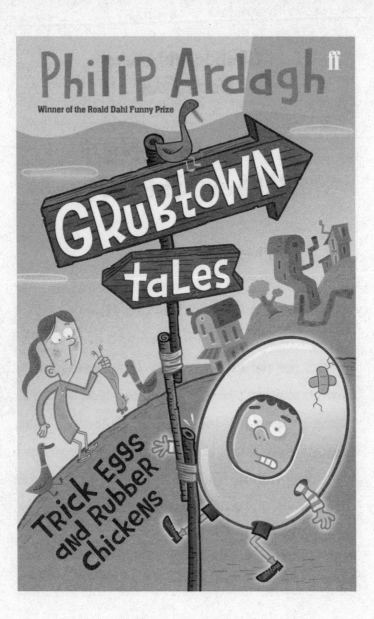

GRuBtoWN taLes
Book Five

TRick Eggs aNd RubbeR ChickeNs

or

Making a Splash

Everything in Grubtown should be very lovely. Mayor Flabby Gomez has finally finished knitting his new house, and the brand new Grubtown Aquarium and Carwash is about to open its leaky doors . . . but with the duck-hating Fox family out for revenge and some seriously dodgy dealings, things are about to get about as crazy as the townsfolk!

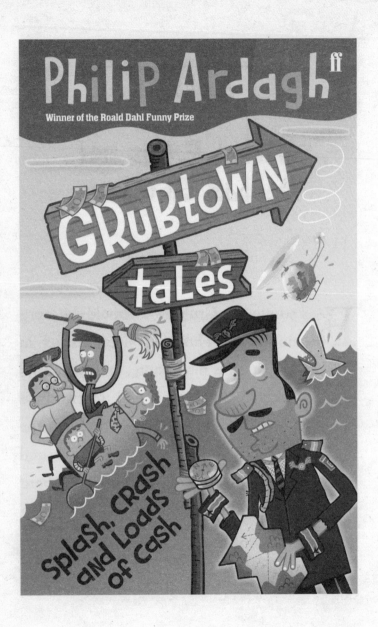

GRuBtoWN taLes
Book Six

Splash, CRash aNd LoadS of Cash

or

In Very Deep Water

When a yachting trip turns to disaster and the shipwrecked crew, including Mango Claptrap, ends up using the impressively large Mayor Flabby Gomez as a man-made floating island, they need help. Who better to rescue them than the exceedingly useless lifeboat crew over at Limp, assisted by Grubtown's very own chief of police, Grabby Hanson? Just about anyone, actually, for they have problems of their own. It's down to Jilly to try to save the day, and to avoid those circling sharks!